This book belongs to my friend:

AUG

A NOTE TO PARENTS

In *Dora's Shape Adventure*, Dora and Boots unravel a set of clues involving shapes in order to reach a friend who needs their help. Your child will enjoy deciphering the clues and at the same time will practice shape identification and Spanish language skills.

As Dora and Boots come upon each rhyming clue, ask your child to find the answers in the accompanying picture before turning the page to reveal the answers. Once your child points out the shapes that solve the clues, ask him to guess how the shapes will assist Dora and Boots. For example, "What object can be formed from a triangle and a crescent that will aid them in their journey?" The first few times you read the story, read both the English and Spanish shape words; then read only one set of words, and ask your child to try to translate.

Continue exploring shapes by pointing out all the different shapes in your home. Challenge your child to find an object that matches each of the shapes in *Dora's Shape Adventure*. You can also bake shapes. Using basic sugar cookie dough and a plastic knife, cut out various shapes with cookie cutters. Then bake, decorate, and enjoy!

Learning Fundamental:  **color + shape**

For more parent and kid-friendly activities, go to **www.nickjr.com**.

Dora's Shape Adventure

ENGLISH/SPANISH GLOSSARY and PRONUNCIATION GUIDE

English	Spanish	Pronunciation
Diamond	El rombo	EL RROM-boh
Let's go!	¡Vámonos!	BAH-moh-nohs
Hello	Hola	OH-lah
Triangle	El triángulo	EL tree-AN-goo-loh
Circle	El círculo	EL SEER-coo-loh
Square	El cuadrado	EL kwah-DRAH-doh
Crescent	El semicírculo	EL seh-mee-SEER-coo-loh
Rectangle	El rectángulo	EL rrec-TAN-goo-loh
Oval	El óvalo	EL OH-bah-loh
One	Uno	OO-noh
Two	Dos	DOHS
Three	Tres	TREHS
Thank you	Gracias	GRAH-see-ahs
You're welcome	De nada	deh NAH-dah
Good-bye	Adiós	ah-dee-OHS

Published by Scholastic Inc., 90 Old Sherman Turnpike, Danbury, CT 06816

SCHOLASTIC and associated logos are trademarks and/or registered trademarks of Scholastic Inc.

ISBN 0-7172-6632-X

Printed in the U.S.A.

First Scholastic Printing, April 2003

Dora's Shape Adventure

by
Susan Hood

illustrated by
**Steve Savitsky
and Arik Roper**

SCHOLASTIC INC.

New York   Toronto   London   Auckland   Sydney
Mexico City   New Delhi   Hong Kong   Buenos Aires

One day, Dora was reading a story to Boots. "In a faraway place called Shape World, there lived a little boy named Pedro. Pedro's favorite toy was a diamond-shaped kite.

One afternoon, a fine breeze was blowing. So Pedro took his kite outside, and it sailed up, up, up into the sky! But suddenly the wind changed, and the kite flew into the branches of a tall tree. Pedro pulled on the string, but the kite wouldn't move. It was stuck!

'Help!' My kite!' cried Pedro. 'How will I get it loose?'"

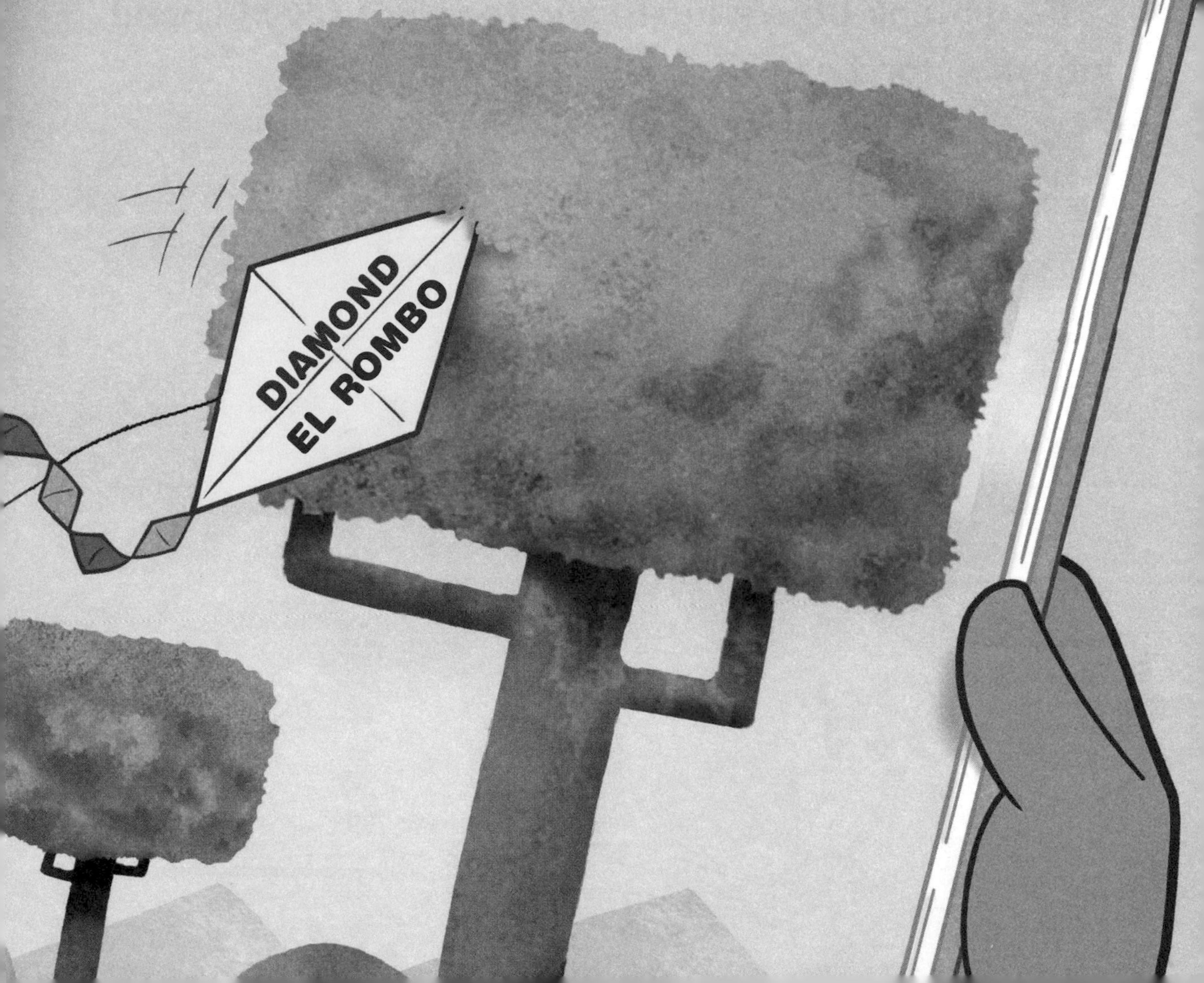

"Boots, Pedro needs our help!" Dora shouted. "¡Vámonos!"

"Hooray, let's go, Dora!" Boots agreed.

Boots took Dora's hand, and together they jumped into the storybook!

Dora and Boots landed in Shape World!
"How do we find Pedro?" Boots wondered.
"Let's ask Map!" Dora suggested.
"Map! Map!" they called. Map hopped right out of
Backpack's side pocket.

"*Hola,* Map," said Dora. "Can you help us find Pedro?"

"No problem," said Map. "First you go over Triangle Mountain, then across Circle Lake, and then through Square Gate. That's how you'll find Pedro."

Dora looked around. "There are some mountains!" she said. "But which one is Triangle Mountain?"

"It's the one that's pointy on top!" Boots exclaimed.
"You're right!" said Dora. "But how do we get over it?"
Suddenly the book in Dora's hand flopped open.

"Boots! There's a message on the page!" said Dora. "Listen:

If you want to fly through the air,
Look for a circle with a square.

Do you see a circle and a square?" Dora asked.

TRIANGLE
EL TRIÁNGULO

"There! A hot air balloon!" shouted Boots.

"Yes, that's a circle and a square!" Dora said excitedly. "And a hot air balloon can fly through the air."

The two friends jumped into the balloon, and soon they were flying over Triangle Mountain.

Boots looked at all the shapes below. "Where do we go next, Dora?" he asked.

Dora repeated Map's directions, "Triangle Mountain, Circle Lake, Square Gate . . . Circle Lake is next."

"Look, Dora!" shouted Boots. "There are three lakes. Which one is Circle Lake?"

Dora pointed at the round lake in the middle. The hot air balloon landed right beside it.

"This is it!" Boots exclaimed. "But how do we get across the lake?"

With a flap, the book opened to a new page. Dora
read the message to Boots:

"A crescent and a triangle will take
You right across Circle Lake.
Do you see a crescent and a triangle?" she asked.

"I see a raft," said Boots. "But it's shaped like a rectangle, not a triangle."

"Look, Boots!" called Dora. "That boat is shaped like a crescent. And it has a sail that's shaped like a triangle!"

"Let's go!" said Boots.

TRIANGLE
EL TRIÁNGULO

CRESCENT
EL SEMICÍRCULO

**Soon they were sailing across Circle Lake.
"Square Gate is next!" called Dora.**

In a little while, Dora and Boots came to a large wall with three gates.

"Which one is Square Gate?" asked Dora.

"The red one is round, and the yellow one has three sides," said Boots.

"The blue one has four sides that are all the same," Dora said. "This must be Square Gate!"

Boots tried to open the gate.
"Oh, no, it's locked," he groaned.
"How do we open it?"

Flip, flip, flip went the pages of the book. Dora read out loud:

"*Find an oval and a rectangle, too,*
To open the door and let you through.
Do you see a rectangle or an oval?" Dora asked.

"There's an oval!" said Boots, pointing at a hole in a tree.

Dora reached into the hole and pulled out a box. "And this is a rectangle," she said. She opened it. Inside was a large shiny key.

OVAL
EL ÓVALO

RECTANGLE
EL
RECTÁNGULO

"Wow!" shouted Boots. "Let's try it!" He fit the key
into the lock. The gate opened.

There stood Pedro, still holding the kite's string.
He waved sadly to Dora and Boots. "My kite is stuck,"
he told them. "I don't think I'll ever get it back."

"Don't worry, Pedro," said Dora. "I'll bet there's something in Backpack we can use."

"Backpack! Backpack!" Dora and Boots called. "We need something to help us climb this tree!"

What could they use?

Dora climbed up the ladder and through the branches. She reached up as high as she could and caught hold of the kite's string.

Dora took a deep breath and counted to three: "*Uno, dos, tres!*" Then she tugged gently on the string, and the kite dropped right into her hand! "I've got it!" Dora called down to Pedro and Boots.

Dora climbed down the ladder and handed the kite to Pedro.

"*Gracias!*" Pedro exclaimed. "Thank you for rescuing my kite!"

"*De nada,*" said Dora. "You're welcome!"

"Would you like to fly my kite with me?" Pedro asked shyly.

"We'd love to!" laughed Dora and Boots.

And the three friends ran off with Pedro's kite sailing up, up, up into the sky.